uck

d

swimming beach & dock

x bench
x bench
x bench

Sand Hill

shack

Triangle

waterthrush pool

Elm Row

Starker's Point

x bench

Birch Pothole

The Birch Row

Gilbert's Island

x bench

Hickory →

The Ring Around

x bench

Haystack Planting

The gate

Lower Gate

deer trail

Lower Prairie

footbridge

Blind
x

The Ditch

Aldo Leopold's Shack

Aldo Leopold's Shack
Nina's Story

by Nancy Nye Hunt

with a foreword by Nina Leopold Bradley

and original illustrations by Earl J. Madden

Center Books on American Places

George F. Thompson, series founder and director

The Center for American Places
at Columbia College Chicago

Mitakuye Oyasin

For all my relatives past, present, and future,
especially Tom, Alison, and Emily, and for Nina, Trish, and Haley

Contents

Foreword

Dear Readers,

Can you imagine buying a piece of land because it had been destroyed and then abandoned by the previous owner? That is just what my father and mother, Aldo and Estella Leopold, did when they bought a farm along the Wisconsin River, near Baraboo, Wisconsin, in 1935.

The farmhouse had burned down, and only one building remained—an old chicken coop, which we soon called the Shack. We worked to clean it up and to build a bunkhouse where we could sleep. It was fun for all of us—our parents and my three brothers, Starker, Luna, and Carl, and my sister, Estella.

The stories in my father's book, *A Sand County Almanac and Sketches Here and There,* tell how we all worked to bring the land back to health. As we worked, we learned much about the land. We planted trees, prairie grasses, and flowers.

Every weekend we came from our home in Madison to our Shack. We played. We sang together. We learned the names of the birds and watched the plants grow. To us, learning about the land soon became loving the land!

I hope you enjoy these stories about how we Leopold children grew up and how we learned to love the land, just like our parents did. Of all the wonderful books written about my father, Aldo, and the Shack, this book has become my favorite. Why? Because it captures the *spirit* of the place! After reading this book, you'll know just what it felt like to be a kid who grew up at the Shack.

Nina Leopold Bradley
Leopold Preserve, Baraboo, Wisconsin

Prologue

I am a lucky person, for I have come to know Nina Leopold Bradley and her family. As we became friends, we realized we had much in common, including a love of the land. It has been my great privilege to have listened to Nina and her family as they have shared their memories of the Shack.

Nina's father, Aldo Leopold, wrote a now-famous book called *A Sand County Almanac and Sketches Here and There*, first published in 1949 and still in print. It was based on the journals that he wrote at the Shack, with the help of his children. Since then, his teachings and ideas about our relationship with the land (called a *land ethic*) and how to observe changes in nature (called *phenology*) have become known throughout the world. And the Shack has become a national historic landmark, a vital and important place to those who appreciate Aldo Leopold's belief that the land is a community and a home not only for plants and animals, but also for people.

Aldo Leopold is regarded as one of the world's greatest conservationists and teachers. He was a co-founder of the Wilderness Society and pioneered the field of ecology. In every way, he led by example, and he passed along the skills of keen observation and scientific curiosity to his five children: Starker, Luna, Nina, Carl, and Estella. All of this was possible because his wife, Estella, shared his devotion to the land. They both imparted the importance of working and caring not only for each other, but also for the land, no matter where we live.

Here, then, is Nina's story about their life at the Shack.

Nancy Nye Hunt
Prairie Trace Farm, Iowa County, Wisconsin

Aldo Leopold's Shack

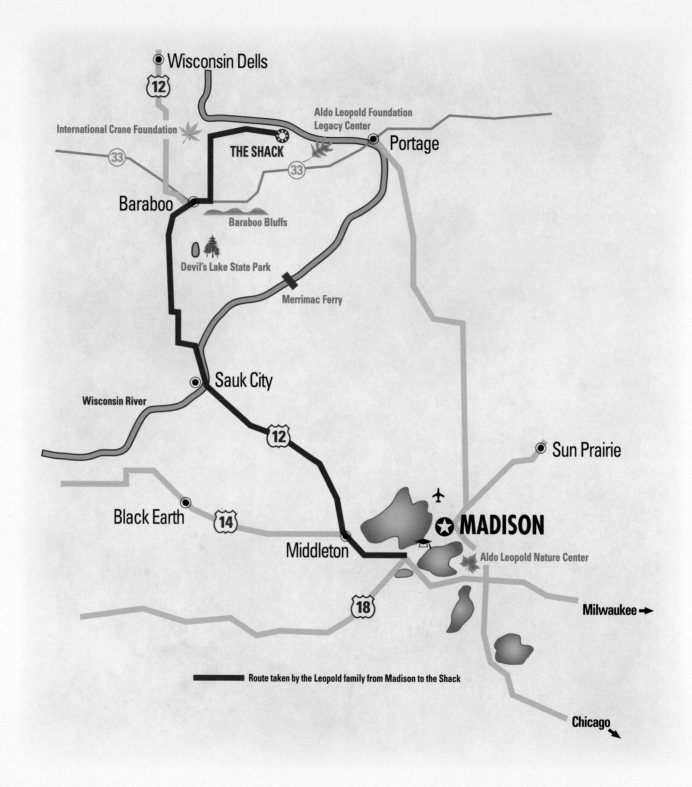

Wisconsin Dells

12

International Crane Foundation

THE SHACK

Aldo Leopold Foundation
Legacy Center

Portage

33

33

Baraboo

Baraboo Bluffs

Devil's Lake State Park

Merrimac Ferry

Sauk City

Wisconsin River

12

Sun Prairie

Black Earth

14

MADISON

Middleton

Aldo Leopold Nature Center

18

Milwaukee →

Chicago

Route taken by the Leopold family from Madison to the Shack

Finding the Shack

Nina was beside herself with excitement.
Around the supper table one winter evening, her father, Aldo Leopold, said, "Mother and I have found an eighty-acre farm in the sand counties of central Wisconsin. We'll be taking a trip there tomorrow."

There was a hush in the room. "Would anyone like to come along?"

Nina, her three brothers, Starker, Luna, and Carl, and her sister, Estella, all chimed in, "We would!" Even their dog, Gus, barked excitedly.

The next day was bright and cold. Mother packed a picnic lunch. Everyone, including Gus, scrambled into the Leopold's little car.

Nina was cozy at first, even though their car didn't have a heater. By the time Nina and her family got to the town of Baraboo, however, they were nearly frozen.

Before they reached the farm, they stopped at their new neighbor's house. His name was Mr. Lewis, and he built a warm fire for them. Soon, Nina's spirits were rekindled, and the last two miles sped by. Nina couldn't wait to see their new land.

Dad turned in at an old gate. He guided the car down a wind-swept driveway lined with skeletal elms. At the end of the lane, Nina hopped out only to stop, frozen in her tracks.

She saw a desolate wasteland. Corn stubble and cocklebur poked at her feet. "What a grim and awful-looking place," she thought. "This land is a disaster!"

She blew warmth into her mittens and whispered, "Our sand county farm has been used up and forgotten."

Nina looked behind her and saw her brothers and sister staring speechless at an old, rundown chicken coop. Luna grumbled, "What a funny, broken-down little shack!" Nina turned to see her mother and father. They were holding hands, gazing across the abandoned landscape.

Dad suddenly exclaimed, "You can see the health of the land is gone. I wonder how long it took a farmer to use it all up?" He paused thoughtfully. "I wonder which plants and animals were here before the farmer?" Then he added, "I think, if we work together, we can restore this worn-out farm!"

Despite the cold, Nina warmed up to his ideas. She began to sense the history of the place and knew Dad would have important plans for its future.

"Woof!" Gus barked.

Her brother, Starker, laughed, "Let's clean up this old shack." They pried open the door.

"This floor is covered in musty old chicken manure!" her brother, Carl, declared. It didn't take long for Nina's family to shovel and scrape the floor clean.

After they washed up, everyone joined Mother and huddled together on a blanket under the elms for their first meal at the Shack. Her warm Spanish meatballs, called *albondigas,* along with cornbread and honey, never tasted so good!

During a walk that afternoon, when the sun dipped low in the west, Nina discovered fresh fox tracks in the snow along the frozen banks of the Wisconsin River. Chickadees whistled the last of the day's friendly calls.

Nina stood still and closed her eyes. The cold air swept across her face. Nina made a quiet promise to learn what she could from this new place.

On the ride home to Madison that starry, winter night, Nina listened contentedly to Dad and Mother sharing their ideas about how the family could heal the land. Nina smiled inside. She couldn't wait to get started.

Improving the Shack

During the next few years, the Leopolds worked hard at the Shack. Everyone pitched in to make changes so they could live there while they worked.

Carl and Starker designed an outhouse. Dad purchased lumber in nearby Baraboo because they wanted to build it right away.

Nina and her sister, Estella, were stacking wood for the outdoor cook fire when Starker strode over and declared, "It's as beautiful as the Parthenon!" The girls gazed at the new edifice and giggled.

For other building projects Nina's family ventured upriver in warmer weather, gathering stray pieces of lumber heaved up on shore once the winter ice melted. The oak slabs and cottonwood planks were bundled together.

"We need to float these downriver to the Shack," Dad said.

Nina, her brothers, and her sister all gleefully jumped into the Wisconsin River. Riding atop the wooden bundles, they floated back to the Shack.

Nina held tightly to the water-soaked wood. The cool, swiftly moving water carried her through the sparkling, sunlit waves. Suddenly, fifteen Canada geese flew low over the river. The Leopold children let out a whoop, and the geese honked back!

When Nina looked behind her, she was surprised. Bobbing in the river and riding atop a large log was her sister, Estella, who proclaimed, "I name this log, Napoleon!" When they all arrived at the beach, Estella pulled the log back upriver and rode it down again and again!

Everyone carried the wood up to the Shack. The "Napoleon" log became the base of a table when a flat plank was put on top. A long slab of oak that had been an old bridge piling was attached to a whitewashed wall inside the Shack. It doubled as a bench and a shelf.

Dad fashioned a split piece of wood into an outside bench. It would become one of his favorite places to sit. There he would organize and review his field notes at the end of the day. Then he would enter the notes into the Shack journals.

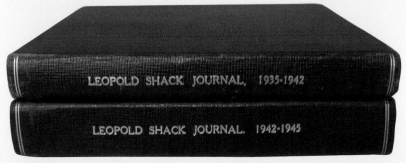

In the darkening twilight, spring peeper frogs serenaded Mother as she laid out the family's bedrolls on the ground around the campfire. Nina watched her straighten up and gaze at the Shack.

"With all of the wood we've collected," Mother said, "we ought to build a bunkhouse onto the Shack."

Nina liked that idea. "Then we'd stay warm and dry in all kinds of weather," she said.

The weather was cold and nasty the week that Nina's family built the bunkhouse. It was tough to drive nails into the cottonwood planks.

When the outside was completed, Dad said, "Starker, would you help me string two layers of wooden snow fence inside to make the upper and lower bunks?"

Mother added, "The rest of us can gather marsh hay near Lake Chapman. We can load it on top of the car, drive it back to the Shack, and then place it on the snow fence for bedding."

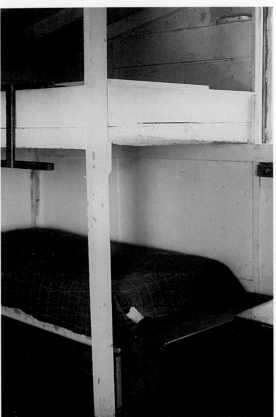

The next big project was to build an indoor fireplace to keep themselves warm. Luna designed it, and Dad and Starker helped to build it. At first, the new fireplace billowed smoke into the Shack and chased everyone outside.

Dad and Luna added an extension onto the chimney, hoping to draw up the smoke. But that didn't work either! Luna was determined to solve the problem.

With much planning and effort, Luna designed a bigger fireplace, using a large, very heavy limestone slab. Luna needed gravel to mix concrete for the new fireplace.

Working outside, he asked, "Nina, will you pump water and wash gravel on this screen?" He turned to Estella. "You can collect the gravel into the old farmhouse sink." He added, "Then we can all take turns mixing the gravel with cement and sand to make concrete."

Putting a red cedar mantle in place was the finishing touch. Now all that was left was to wait for it to dry and harden.

Mother lit the oil lamps and placed them on the new mantle. Dad put wood in the fireplace, and Luna lit a match.

Everyone was excited to see if Luna's efforts had worked. Flames quickly crackled to life, but wisps of smoke still crept into the room.

Dad and Mother smiled. Nina and Estella grinned. Carl and Starker laughed. Luna was quiet. He was disappointed that the fireplace wasn't working as it should, and he scowled as a trace of smoke curled around his head.

"You've built a beautiful fireplace, Luna," Mother declared, trying to comfort him. "Now let's make supper!"

Mother always packed enough chuck, or provisions, to last for the duration of their visits.

She worked hard all day, but, in the evenings, Dad treated her like a Spanish princess. He and the children cooked supper while she relaxed and enjoyed the day's conversations either outside under the elms or inside next to the fireplace.

Corrected Chuck List
for
Current River Trip Nov. 27 – Dec. 7, 1926
(3 men 10 days)

1½ lbs.	Crisco	10 cans milk, small
6 "	bacon	1½ lbs. coffee
3 "	ham	3 pints jam
2 doz.	eggs	2 lbs. fruit cake
2 lbs.	butter	2 " cookies
2 "	kraft cheese	1 " tobacco
4 oz.	Baking powder	1 box matches in tin
15 lbs.	flour	6 miner's candles & open-neck bottle for holder
1 pkg.	Rye Crisp	2 doz. peanut bars
5 lbs.	cornmeal	3 oz. tea
1 lb.	hominy	4 oz. cocoa
2 lbs.	noodles	2 qts. syrup
1 lb.	rice	2 bars soap
2 lbs.	macaroni	2 yds. cheesecloth
8 "	potatoes	
4 "	sweet potatoes	

Utensils

Nested outfit – (Coffee pot (2 kettles (5 cups

1 doz.	onions
3 lbs.	navy beans
2 oz.	soda in special can
2 lbs.	seeded raisins
3 "	prunes & peaches
7 "	apples
5 "	sugar
½ "	salt

1 Sourdough kettle

1 Dutch oven

1 fry pan, 4 plates, forks, spoons.

1 large spoon

Cake knife, camp knife, pliers, can opener.

1 canvas bucket

Food bags

Suspended over the fire by sturdy, wrought iron hangers, hearty stews bubbled in open pots while Mother's cornbread baked in Dutch ovens. Nina set the table with Blue Willow plates and mugs.

Mother's Cornbread

1 cup of flour
2 cups of cornmeal
3 tablespoons of sugar
1 teaspoon of salt
1 teaspoon of baking powder

1 egg
¼ cup oil
About 1 cup of milk or water to make a runny paste

In a large mixing bowl, stir together the flour, cornmeal, sugar, salt, and baking powder. Make a well in the center of the dry mixture. In a medium mixing bowl, combine the egg, milk, and oil. Add the egg mixture to the dry mixture all at once (in the center of the well). Stir just until moistened (the batter should be lumpy). Pour the batter into a Dutch oven or square pan. Follow these baking instructions:

For a Dutch oven: Grease a ten-inch Dutch oven and its top and preheat over the coals. Remove from the coals. Pour the batter into the Dutch oven. Place the lid on top. Put the Dutch oven next to the coals. Put more coals on top of the lid. Turn the Dutch oven one-third of the way every seven minutes for a total of twenty minutes or until golden brown. Remove the cornbread immediately from the oven.

For a conventional oven: Grease an eight-inch square baking pan. Pour the batter into the pan. Bake at 425º for twenty to twenty-five minutes. Cut into squares. Makes nine servings.

23

The whole family took turns tidying up after every meal. Water came from the outdoor pump and was heated over the fire. The pots, pans, and dishes were then washed and rinsed in two large, white enamel bowls.

Nina often watched Dad, pipe in mouth, absentmindedly dry the dishes. She could tell by his far-off gaze that he was deep in thought.

Routinely every evening, Dad would reach into his shirt pocket, remove his tiny packet of field notes, and begin copying his observations into the Shack journals by firelight.

west and began "using" over our meadow (just as Silvia had predicted) so we came on in.

Duck tally:

No.	Species	Sex	Age	Notes
1	Woodduck	♂	Young	Full adult male plumage (no quill vestiges). Crop crammed with acorns.
2	Woodduck	♀	Young	Crop also full of acorns (black oak ?). We counted 23 full acorns, in hulls.
3	Woodduck	♀	Young	Over half juvenal plumage; quite young.
4	Green wing teal	♂	Young	Only traces of drake plumage were a few vermiculated feathers on flanks.
5	Blue winged teal	♂	Young	Greater secondary coverts — white
6	Blue winged teal	♀	Young	Greater sec. coverts — black with white outer edge and one transverse white bar.
7	Pintail	♂	Adult	Just changing from eclipse to winter plumage. Molt starts on belly and flanks, works dorsally + forward.

Sexual differences in greater secondary coverts of
Blue winged teal wings

Young ♀   Young ♂

Mottled   White

"Duérmete Niño"

A la puerta del cielo venden zapatos
Para los angelitos que van descalzos.

Duérmete niño,
Duérmete niño,
Duérmete niño, arru, arru.

A los niños que duermen Dios los bendece.
A las madres que velan Dios las asiste.

Duérmete niño,
Duérmete niño,
Duérmete niño, arru, arru.

"Fall Asleep Child"

At heaven's gate they sell shoes
For the little angels that go barefoot.

Fall asleep child,
Fall asleep child,
Fall asleep child, ah, ah, ah.

God blesses the children that are sleeping.
God blesses the mothers that are watching over.

Fall asleep child,
Fall asleep child,
Fall asleep child, ah, ah, ah.

Often the Leopolds settled in for a good sing after supper. Mother had taught them the old Spanish family songs from New Mexico, where her family first settled during the mid-1600s.

They took turns passing the guitar among them. Nina especially loved when Mother would sing the lullaby, "Duérmete Niño" ("Fall Asleep Child"), at the end of the day.

When the last notes were sung, the Leopold children would race for the upper bunk and nestle into their bedrolls for the night. Nina watched the evening star twinkle through the small window next to her. Sometimes barred owls hooted back and forth as she fell asleep.

Spring

With spring, Nina's family arrived at the Shack in various ways, depending on the weather conditions.

Sometimes they drove right to the Shack through biting blizzards.

Sometimes snowmelt flooded the road, and they could not get the car beyond Mr. Lewis's meadow. Then everyone walked in from the west, carrying their gear and chuck.

Sometimes the Wisconsin River overflowed its banks, flooding their road. Then they rowed a boat across Lake Chapman, coming in from the south. Once their car was pulled out of the mud by a team of horses!

Spring was always a busy time at the Shack. The apple orchard had to be pruned and tended. The food patch had to be plowed and planted with tomatoes, potatoes, onions, melons, and peas. Even a grape arbor was started.

The family replanted prairies with native wildflowers and grasses and noted spring bloom times. And each year they planted thousands of young Norway, jack, and white pines. On occasion, hundreds of the trees might perish from drought or be eaten by deer or rabbits. But each spring Nina and her family kept planting more seedlings, always hopeful some would become tall trees.

There was also much to observe during spring migration. The river was crowded with ducks, geese, gulls, and even cormorants. A variety of hawks flew overhead.

The family caught and banded chickadees, identifying them as individuals and locating their return on maps.

Nina and her family saw the reappearance of sandhill cranes in Wisconsin! The cranes, an ancient species, were one of Dad's favorites.

Dad enjoyed reading the notations the children made in the Shack journals. One evening Nina wrote, "We heard two woodcock peenting and snipe winnowing. The trees were filled with myrtle warblers."

Nina used words that sounded like the territorial calls that birds make. She learned them by watching Dad study the behavior of birds and then record what he saw and heard in the journals.

Once, after a long day of working, Nina and Dad walked back along the road. Suddenly, at the woods' edge, out of a leaf-covered brush pile, a woodcock flushed, pretending to be hurt.

Nina whispered, "It's hopping away, but it keeps looking back at us."

Dad silently pointed to the brush pile and soon located a nest with four eggs. "Look," he said. "She's protecting the nest by drawing our attention away from it."

At twilight, Nina and Carl raced to the woodcock peenting grounds north of the Shack to watch a "skydance." Breathlessly, Nina said, "Listen, there it is!"

A woodcock was grunting and peenting. Its courtship dance began. The bird circled up into the darkening sky.

Nina and Carl raced to the area and quickly laid on the cool grass. They waited, their hearts beating rapidly.

Twittering and chirping, the woodcock rose higher, then silently plummeted straight to the ground very close to Nina and Carl, only to begin again. A cool breeze blew in from the west, but Nina and Carl barely noticed. In the dim light, Nina looked at her watch. That night, the "skydance" lasted one hour.

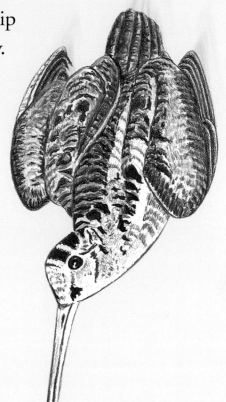

Summer

Longer days announced the arrival of summer.
Whenever the family arrived at the Shack, the Leopold children
made the full circuit to check up on the land: they ran west,
then south, and then north back to the Shack. Along the way,
they raced to see who could find the tallest tree from their
previous plantings. "Look," Estella cried, "This one is up
to my waist!"

There were always so many fun things to do. The children swam in and canoed the Wisconsin River, had long-jump contests on the sandy beach, roamed the woods with Gus, and fished for bass and pike on Lake Chapman.

41

One summer Luna built a tree house in a stately elm behind the Shack. After it was finished, Nina climbed up, holding the family songbook.

"Tie the rope to the guitar, Estella," Nina called down. She then hauled up the guitar, and Estella scurried up the tree after it.

They spent the entire day learning an old Spanish song, "Naranja Dulce" or "Sweet Orange," until an afternoon rainstorm sent them inside.

On clear evenings, the family sat outside, having a good sing. The old family songs mingled with the night sounds. But the gathering swarms of mosquitoes eventually drove them all inside.

"Naranja Dulce"

Naranja dulce, limón partido
Dame un abrazo
Por Dios te pido
Si fueron falsos mis juramentos
En otros tiempos, es un olvidar.

"Sweet Orange"

Sweet orange, divided lemon
Give me a hug
I ask you on behalf of God
If my oaths were false
In other times, it is forgotten.

Occasionally, when Nina awakened before dawn, she looked out her window beside the bunk. She could barely see Dad sitting on a bench.

At the first hint of daylight, he tilted his head, looked at his watch, and made notations. Nina heard an indigo bunting and knew Dad was noting the order of birdsongs with the increasing light.

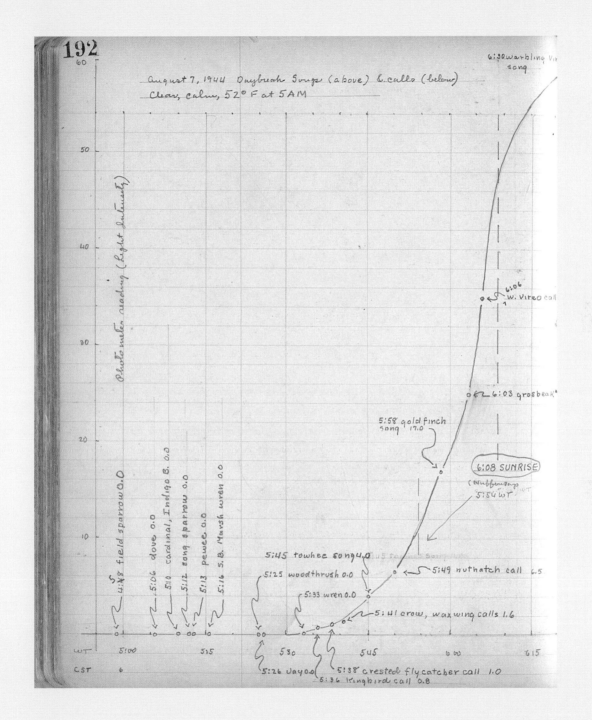

August 7, 1944   Daybreak Songs (above) & calls (below)
Clear, calm, 52° F at 5 AM

6:30 warbling Vireo song

6:06 w. Vireo call

6:03 grosbeak

5:58 goldfinch song 17.0

6:08 SUNRISE

5:54 WT

5:45 towhee song 4.0

5:25 woodthrush 0.0

5:33 wren 0.0

5:49 nuthatch call 6.5

5:41 crow, waxwing calls 1.6

Photo meter reading (light intensity)

4:48 field sparrow 0.0

5:06 dove 0.0

5:10 cardinal, Indigo B. 0.0

5:12 song sparrow 0.0

5:13 Pewee 0.0

5:16 S.B. Marsh wren 0.0

60

50

40

30

20

10

WT   5:00   5:15   5:30   5:45   6:00   6:15

CST   6

5:26 Jay 0.0

5:38 crested flycatcher call 1.0
5:36 Kingbird call 0.8

When Dad came back in, it meant one thing: sourdough pancakes! Everyone pitched in. Soon bacon, eggs, and pancakes were sizzling over the fire. The hot pancakes were rolled up with the bacon tucked inside. They disappeared quickly!

The Family's Sourdough Pancakes

The night before:
Dissolve 2½ teaspoons of yeast in 1 cup of warm water. Whisk in 1 cup of flour. Take it to bed with you to keep it warm.

In the morning:
Add:
1 egg
1 teaspoon of baking soda
2 tablespoons of sugar
½ teaspoon of salt

Lightly whisk just to mix. Let it sit twenty minutes. Grease and preheat a ten-inch skillet. Use about ¼ cup of batter to make an eight-inch pancake. Pour in the batter and roll around the pan so it is thin. When the bubbles have popped and the top is dry, flip it over.
　　Makes eight to ten pancakes. To serve: add butter and put bacon, sausage, or cinnamon sugar on top. Roll up the pancake. Add maple syrup. Enjoy!

48

Autumn

The golden days of autumn brought many changes to the land. Animals were on the move. Skunks, foxes, and deer left tracks near the Shack. Migrating birds gathered along the river. Nina heard the ancient call of sandhill cranes flying south on their way to their winter home.

Mother harvested the grapes from the arbor and dug the last of the potatoes and onions from the food patch. Birdhouses and nesting boxes were emptied and cleaned. Inside the Shack, leaks were patched, and chinks in the walls were filled in to keep out the cold. Everyone prepared for deer hunting season.

On fall days, the family burned the newly restored prairies, returning nutrients to the soil. One afternoon the Leopolds worked as a team, burning fire lanes around the Shack and yard. "That way," Dad explained, "if a fire were to come close to the Shack, it would stop, because the dry grass has already been burned away in these lanes."

Afterward, Nina called to Carl, "Let's go down to the slough and see what's there."

They ran down Slide Hill through the woods to the backwater of the Wisconsin River. Flick, the family's second dog, was close on their heels.

They stood on the edge of the slough and looked through the woods as dusk settled in. Flick heard them first.

Twenty ducks came in fast and landed right in front of Nina and Carl. "Blue-winged teal," she whispered. "And look, mallards, scaup, and geese."

They came in fours and in eights until the slough was overflowing with splashing and diving ducks and geese. Carl counted 215 of them!

Nina held tightly to Flick. "What a sight," she said softly in his ear. Flick wagged his tail.

The splendid fall days quickly changed whenever a northwestern gale howled around the Shack.

One day a heavy frost coated the last remaining oak leaves. Nina was helping Mother mix cornbread batter when Dad and Carl burst in through the door.

"We cut down an old oak snag along the creek bank!" Carl said breathlessly. "When it fell, the top broke off and dripped honey!"

"Only a few bees came out," Dad added, "Let's go collect some honey, but we'll be sure to leave half, so the bees can have their share over winter." Dad always thought about the needs of wildlife.

54

Winter

All winter long the Leopolds collected firewood.
They trekked into the woods, with saws and axes in hand.
They cut wood all morning, stacking it onto sleds to haul back
to the woodshed.

They ate lunch in the woods, sitting on logs fresh with the
scent of sawdust and woodchips scattered all about. Chickadees
flitted overhead. Nina tossed crumbs from Mother's cornbread
onto the snow. Soon the friendly chickadees sat on her shoulders
and feet. One even ate out of Carl's hand!

After lunch Dad split a piece of ash, which exposed many
ant eggs. The grateful chickadees quickly gobbled up this unusual
winter treat.

On crisp, sunny, winter days, Nina, Carl, and Estella played tracking games. "One, two, three . . ." Nina and Estella counted slowly as Carl ran off into the woods, making tracks in the snow. ". . . 98, 99, 100!" they shouted.

It was easy to follow alongside his tracks in the snow. But soon the tracks mysteriously ended. They looked closely for clues. "He's backtracked!" Nina exclaimed. They traced a little ways back, and then the tracks veered off, ending abruptly at an oak tree. There was Carl high up in the tree, grinning!

Nina's family owned two pairs of cross-country skis, so they all took turns out in the snow. Nina loved to ski with Mother. Sometimes Carl would come, too, wearing his camera around his neck, stopping to snap photographs.

Mother led the way, wearing her long skirt and "Old Faithful." That is what she called her thick, woolen coat. Deep into the woods, Gus and Flick flushed grouse from downed oak snags. Near the slough, they saw mink and muskrat tracks. Even in winter the land was full of life!

One day, with a warm fire crackling away, Nina borrowed Mother's coat, "Old Faithful," and put on a pair of skis. She headed out with Gus and Flick bounding after her. Nina skied past the tree house and up over Sand Hill into the tall oaks. There she glided to a stop.

Nina caught her breath in the cold, clean air. She looked around and thought about all of the changes to the land that had happened since her family came to this old farm years ago. "When we first came here," she confided to the dogs, "this was nothing."

Nina remembered the grim and barren landscape. As she gazed in all directions, she could see the young trees they had planted over the years. She thought of the birds and animals finding new homes in the restored prairies, woodlands, and wetlands that her family worked hard together to create.

Nina remembered all of the fun she had with her parents, her brothers, and her sister. She thought about all she had learned and observed here. "Now this means everything to me," she said aloud.

Through their hard work, Nina and her family had given a lot to the land. But she also realized how much the land had given back to her family. They belonged to this land.

All of a sudden, a chickadee whistled overhead. Nina whistled back and then thought of the good oak burning in the fireplace. She called to the dogs, "Time to head back to our dear little Shack!"

Afterword

Many years have passed since Nina and her family first came to the Shack on a cold, winter day. The farm's once barren landscape is "a desolate wasteland" only in old photographs.

The family's hard work transformed the land. The thousands of trees they planted have grown to maturity. The prairies they restored have flourished. The diversity of plant and animal species has greatly expanded.

The Shack and the surrounding land are now called the Leopold Preserve, and it is a sanctuary for all life-forms that inhabit it. In fact, the Shack is now listed on both the United States Register of Historic Places and the National Register of Historic Landmarks.

Visitors today can still see the unassuming Shack. The Wisconsin River, in all its moods, steadily flows onward past the preserve, and wind whistles through the now towering pines.

Who knows? Sitting quietly on a Leopold bench, one may feel the same inspiration that cultivated the Leopold family's love of nature. And, with luck, a descendant of one of their banded chickadees may sound its friendly call: "Welcome! Welcome to you all!"

Aldo Leopold's Concepts

The Land Ethic

In *A Sand County Almanac and Sketches Here and There* (Oxford University Press, 1949), Aldo Leopold presented an innovative idea called the *land ethic*. He stated that the land—wherever it is—has its own intrinsic value. He defined the land as including soil, water, plants, animals, and people. All of these components form a community of life.

In his view, people have a special ethical obligation in relation to each other, to all life-forms, and to the land. Thus, an individual has a personal responsibility to appreciate, understand, and respect the land as a whole, which ensures the health of the land and, ultimately, the health of the entire community.

Aldo Leopold understood the complex interdependence of all living things, because of his professional life as a forester and wildlife ecologist and through his personal experiences with his family at the Shack. As he famously wrote, "There are two things that interest me: the relation of people to each other and the relation of people to the land." He knew that we could have a better world if we learned to live by the land ethic.

Phenology

Phenology is the study of monitoring changes in nature; that is, recording annual and periodic natural occurrences, such as plant bloom times, bird migrations, and animals emerging from hibernation. The study of phenology especially considers the influence that weather, climate, and seasonal changes have on these events.

Aldo Leopold and his family began recording this data at the Shack in 1936. They noted the spring arrival dates of sandhill cranes, the first bloom of the pasqueflower, and when the painted turtle laid her eggs. They noted when bats departed and when the Wisconsin River froze over.

Nina Leopold Bradley has continued to watch and collect data on the Leopold Preserve, where she has lived since 1976. The longevity of this phenological record has provided a valuable look at changing trends in plant and animal ranges. Thanks to Nina, we now know that some spring events occur earlier than they used to, and some ranges have expanded, very probably in response to climate change and a warmer global environment.

Phenology Record from Bradley Study Center

Recorded by:_____

#	original item name	latin name	earliest	latest	average	2005	Comments
1	Black-capped Chickadee Two-note Song	*Poecile atricapillas*	1-Jan	8-Feb	17-Jan		
2	Striped Skunk First Tracks	*Mephitis mephitis*	3-Jan	4-Mar	4-Feb		
3	Northern Cardinal First Song	*Cardinalis cardinalis*	3-Jan	23-Mar	10-Feb		
315	Tufted Titmouse Spring Arrival	*Baeolophus bicolor*					
4	Wisconsin River Opens	0	1-Jan	31-Mar	29-Feb		
9	Common Goldeneye Spring Arrival	*Bucephala clangula*	20-Jan	28-Mar	1-Mar		
6	Canada Goose Spring Arrival	*Branta canadensis*	25-Jan	3-Apr	5-Mar		
7	Sandhill Crane Spring Arrival	*Grus canadensis*	13-Feb	22-Mar	5-Mar		
8	Northern Harrier First Observation	*Circus cyaneus*	3-Feb	25-Apr	7-Mar		
10	Eastern Bluebird Spring Arrival	*Sialia sialis*	10-Feb	30-Mar	8-Mar		
11	American Robin Spring Arrival	*Turdus migratorius*	2-Feb	30-Mar	10-Mar		
12	Red-Winged Blackbird Spring Arrival	*Agelaius phoeniceus*	25-Feb	2-Apr	14-Mar		
13	Common Grackle Spring Arrival	*Quiscalus quiscula*	4-Mar	27-Mar	14-Mar		
14	Killdeer Spring Arrival	*Charadrius vociferus*	28-Feb	9-Apr	16-Mar		
15	Eastern Meadowlark Spring Arrival	*Sturnella magna*	28-Feb	10-Apr	19-Mar		
16	American Woodcock First Peent	*Scolopax minor*	1-Mar	8-Apr	21-Mar		
17	Song Sparrow Spring Arrival	*Melospiza melodia*	22-Feb	16-Apr	21-Mar		
18	Wood Duck Spring Arrival	*Aix sponsa*	6-Mar	14-Apr	23-Mar		
19	Turkey Vulture Spring Arrival	*Cathartes aura*	11-Feb	17-Apr	24-Mar		
20	Skunk Cabbage 1st Bloom	*Symplocarpus foetidus*	19-Feb	16-Apr	25-Mar		
21	Hooded Merganser Spring Arrival	*Lophodytes cucullatus*	9-Mar	11-Apr	27-Mar		
22	Fox Sparrow Spring Arrival	*Passerella iliaca*	3-Mar	18-Apr	27-Mar		
23	Eastern Phoebe Spring Arrival	*Sayornis phoebe*	12-Mar	20-Apr	28-Mar		
24	Northern Cricket Frog Song	*Acris crepitans crepitans*	20-Mar	7-Apr	29-Mar		
28	Center Pond Ice Free	0	27-Feb	14-Apr	29-Mar		
25	Tundra Swan First Sighting	*Cygnus columbianus*	12-Mar	20-Apr	29-Mar		
27	Great Blue Heron Spring Arrival	*Ardea herodius*	20-Mar	19-Apr	30-Mar		
29	Fool Arrives	0	1-Apr	1-Apr	1-Apr		
30	Eastern Garter Snake First Sighting	*Thamnophis sirtalis sirtalis*	15-Mar	15-Apr	1-Apr		
31	Belted Kingfisher Spring Arrival	*Ceryle alcyon*	5-Mar	21-Apr	2-Apr		

A Brief Chronology of Aldo Leopold's Life
(Used by permission of the Aldo Leopold Foundation.)

1887 Aldo Leopold, born in Burlington, Iowa, on January 11, eldest of the four children of Carl and Clara Leopold.

1904 Attends Lawrenceville School in New Jersey, from January 1904 to May 1905, to prepare for college.

1906 Begins course work at Yale University Forest School (receives a Master of Science of Forestry in 1909).

1909 Joins the U.S. Forest Service (which was established in 1905), with his first field assignment as an assistant in the Apache National Forest in southeastern Arizona.

1911 Transferred to the Carson National Forest in northern New Mexico as Deputy Supervisor, then as Supervisor. Founds and edits *Carson Pine Cone*, a U.S. Forest Service newsletter.

1912 Marries Estella Bergere, of Santa Fe, New Mexico, on October 9. They have five children: Starker, born in 1913; Luna, born in 1915; Nina, born in 1917; Carl, born in 1919; and Estella, born in 1927.

1922 Submits a formal proposal for the administration of the Gila National Forest as a wilderness area (which was administratively designated by the U.S. Forest Service on June 3, 1924).

1924 Accepts a transfer to the U.S. Forest Products Laboratory in Madison, Wisconsin, as Assistant (later Associate) Director.

1928   Leaves the U.S. Forest Service Products Laboratory and U.S. Forest Service to conduct game surveys of Midwestern states as a private consultant.

1933   In July, accepts an appointment as head of the new game management program in the Department of Agricultural Economics at the University of Wisconsin-Madison.

1935   In April, acquires the farm (known as the Shack) along the Wisconsin River near Baraboo that would be the setting for many of the essays in *A Sand County Almanac and Sketches Here and There* (1949).

1939   Becomes Chairman of a new Department of Wildlife Management at the University of Wisconsin-Madison.

1941   Develops his initial plans for a volume of ecological essays.

1947   In December, submits a book manuscript entitled *Great Possessions* to Oxford University Press, which notifies him of acceptance on April 14, 1948.

1948   While helping to fight a grass fire on a neighbor's farm near the Shack, he is stricken by a heart attack and dies on April 21. Burial is in Burlington, Iowa.

1949   Final editing of *Great Possessions* is overseen by his son, Luna B. Leopold, and is published as *A Sand County Almanac and Sketches Here and There*.

2004   Governor James Doyle signs legislation forever making the first weekend in March "Aldo Leopold Weekend" across Wisconsin.

Aldo Leopold and Estella Bergere were married on October 9, 1912, in the Bergere family home (formerly the Otero family home) at 135 Grant Avenue, in Santa Fe, New Mexico. Interestingly, this house is just around the corner from the Georgia O'Keeffe Museum.

Aldo and Estella had five children:

Aldo Starker
b. 1913, Burlington, Iowa

Luna Bergere
b. 1915, Albuquerque, New Mexico

Marie Adelina (Nina)
b. 1917, Albuquerque, New Mexico

Aldo Carl
b. 1919, Albuquerque, New Mexico

Estella Bergere
b. 1927, Madison, Wisconsin

The Leopold and Bergere Family Tree

(according to the Leopold family)

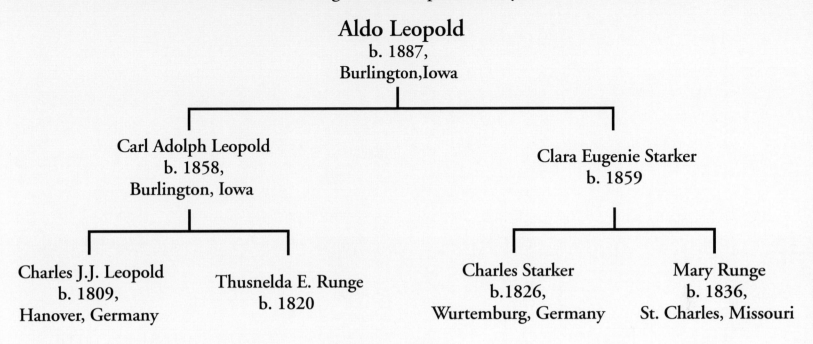

Aldo Leopold
b. 1887,
Burlington, Iowa

Carl Adolph Leopold
b. 1858,
Burlington, Iowa

Clara Eugenie Starker
b. 1859

Charles J.J. Leopold
b. 1809,
Hanover, Germany

Thusnelda E. Runge
b. 1820

Charles Starker
b.1826,
Wurtemburg, Germany

Mary Runge
b. 1836,
St. Charles, Missouri

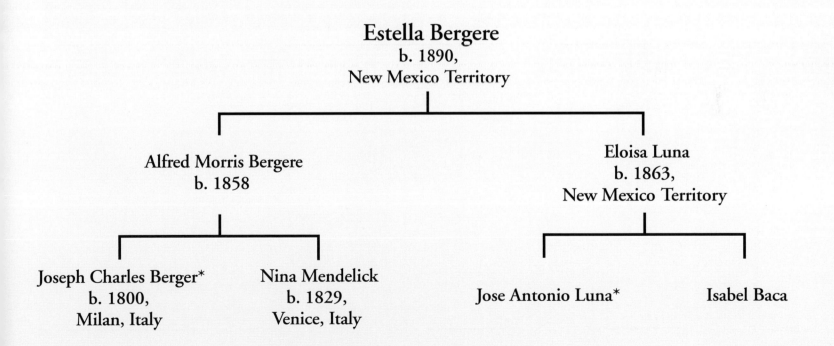

Estella Bergere
b. 1890,
New Mexico Territory

Alfred Morris Bergere
b. 1858

Eloisa Luna
b. 1863,
New Mexico Territory

Joseph Charles Berger*
b. 1800,
Milan, Italy

Nina Mendelick
b. 1829,
Venice, Italy

Jose Antonio Luna*

Isabel Baca

*Names as they appear in the Bergere Family's *Holy Bible*.

Kindred Spirit Organizations

The Aldo Leopold Foundation
P. O. Box 77
Baraboo, WI 53913, U.S.A.
(608) 355-0279
www.aldoleopold.org

Founded in 1982 by Aldo and Estella Leopold's children, the foundation continues to manage the original Leopold farm, which includes the Shack, and to serve as the executor of Aldo Leopold's literary estate. Programs are offered in ecological management and environmental education designed to increase an awareness of and appreciation for the land.

In April 2007, the new Aldo Leopold Legacy Center was completed. Located a mile from the Shack, it was constructed from selectively harvested pines originally planted by the Leopolds. In November 2007, the U.S. Green Building Council recognized the center for being the "greenest" building in the world, noting its innovative energy efficiency techniques (including geothermal) as well as the use of recycled materials and locally harvested wood.

The Aldo Leopold Nature Center
300 Femrite Drive
Monona, WI 53716, U.S.A.
(608) 221-0404
www.naturenet.com/alnc

The Aldo Leopold Nature Center was established in 1994 by Nina Leopold Bradley and others wishing to reconnect children to the land. Since that time, it has become the leading source of Leopold-inspired education for children and families. Its mission is to foster in children a love and respect for the land—and for each other. With learning centers in both urban and rural settings, the Nature Center offers hands-on experiences in the outdoors that, in the words of Aldo Leopold, "teach the student to see the land, understand what he [or she] sees, and enjoy what he [or she] understands."

Visitors can walk the Leopold Family Trail, visit the Children's Shack, explore interactive exhibits (such as "Aldo Leopold as a Boy"), and participate in restoration and learning activities. Recognizing Leopold's belief that "everything is interconnected," the Nature Center also sponsors Nature Net—a consortium of nature centers, zoos, museums, and other organizations working together to connect families to the land.

Index of Illustrations

All historic black-and-white photographs were taken by Carl Leopold, except as noted. They appear courtesy of the Aldo Leopold Foundation in Baraboo, Wisconsin, and the University of Wisconsin-Madison Archives. All contemporary color photographs were taken by the author, except as noted. Aldo Leopold and his wife, Estella Bergere Leopold, are denoted as AL and EBL, respectively, in the descriptions.

Acknowledgments

Many thanks to Nina, Carl, and Estella, for sharing their memories and stories, and to Nina's daughter and son-in-law, Trish and Gordon Stevenson, for their encouragement, friendship, and shared adventures at the Shack. Thanks to Luna's daughter, Madelyn Leopold, for sharing the Bergere family's *Holy Bible* and other genealogical information. Thanks to Susan Flader and the Aldo Leopold Foundation, for the use of archived materials and family photos. Thanks to Bernie Schermetzler, of the University of Wisconsin-Madison Archives, for access and guidance to the Aldo Leopold collection, including the original Shack journals, to the Department of Forest and Wildlife Ecology at the University of Wisconsin-Madison, and to Jaime Stoltenberg, of the Robinson Map Library in the Department of Geography at the University of Wisconsin-Madison. Thanks to the manuscript readers, for their professional insights. They are Wisconsin educators Renice Konik, Chris Charleson, Marlene Ross, and Cathy Wilson; author and conservationist Charles E. Little; and Kathe Crowley Conn, President and Executive Director of the Aldo Leopold Nature Center. Thanks to Spanish teacher Gene Gilbert, of Interlaken, New Jersey, for her translation of the Spanish songs "Duérmete Niño" and "Naranja Dulce." Thanks to Earl J. Madden, for his original illustrations and wonderful book design. Special thanks to Dr. Tom Hunt, for his ideas and, as always, his support, to Alison Drew Hunt, for her skilled copyediting, and to Emily Nye Hunt, for her beautiful photography and computer skills. Finally, a thousand thanks to George F. Thompson, my talented, wise, and accomplished publisher and friend.

About the Author

Nancy Nye Hunt was born and raised in Wisconsin. She fell in love with the land as a child roaming the woods at her grandparents' home near Cedarburg, Wisconsin. After receiving her B.S. in agricultural education at the University of Wisconsin–Madison, she worked as a legislative liaison for the governor, attorney general, and state legislature of Wisconsin. She then was a volunteer and substitute teacher in the elementary schools of Monona, Wisconsin, and worked as a specialist in children's literature at Madison's Pooh Corner bookstore. The mother of two adult daughters, she lives and writes from her home, Prairie Trace Farm, in Wisconsin's Driftless area with her husband, Tom, a professor of restoration ecology, three dogs, two cats, and a frog. This is her first book.

About the Book

Aldo Leopold's Shack: Nina's Story is the twenty-first volume in the *Center Books on American Places* series, George F. Thompson, series founder and director. The book was issued in a hardcover edition of 1,250 copies with the generous financial assistance of the Pleasant T. Rowland Foundation, Nina Leopold Bradley, Gaynor Cranberry Company, Carl Korfmacher, Ken Kruger, Landmark Services Cooperative and CHS Inc., Estella Leopold, Rett Nelson, John and Beth Ross, Scott and Heidi Catlin Schaeffer, Trish and Gordon Stevenson, and others, for which the publisher is most grateful. The text was set in Garamond, the paper is 140 gsm weight, and the book was printed and bound in China. For more information about the Center for American Places at Columbia College Chicago, please see page 84.

For the Center for American Places at Columbia College Chicago:

Special Acknowledgment:
The Center for American Places extends its utmost gratitude to David Douglas and the Wallace Genetic Foundation, for their early and magnanimous support of the Center's goal of bringing to publication important books about places intended for young readers.

George F. Thompson, Founder and Director
Jason Stauter, Operations and Marketing Manager
Erin F. Fearing, Executive Assistant
Alison Drew Hunt, Manuscript Editor
Emily Nye Hunt, Production Assistant
Kate Coughlin, Chelsea Miller Goin Intern
Earl J. Madden, Book Designer and Illustrator
David Skolkin, Art Director

Published in 2011. First edition.
Printed in China on acid-free paper.

The Center for American Places at Columbia College Chicago
600 South Michigan Avenue
Chicago, Illinois 60605-1996, U.S.A.
www.americanplaces.org

Distributed by the University of Chicago Press
www.press.uchicago.edu

19 18 17 16 15 14 13 12 11   1 2 3 4 5

Library of Congress Cataloging-in-Publication Data

Hunt, Nancy Nye, 1953-
  Aldo Leopold's shack : Nina's story / Nancy Nye Hunt.
      p. cm. -- (Center books on American places ; [21])
  ISBN 978-1-935195-17-7
  1. Leopold, Aldo, 1886-1948—Homes and haunts—Juvenile literature.
2. Bradley, Nina Leopold, 1917—Childhood and youth--Juvenile
literature. 3. Naturalists—Wisconsin—Biography—Juvenile literature. 4.
Farm life—Wisconsin—Baraboo Region—Juvenile literature. I. Bradley,
Nina Leopold, 1917- II. Title. III. Series.

  QH31.L618H86 2011
  508.775'76—dc22

                        2010020063

ISBN-13: 978-1-935195-17-7

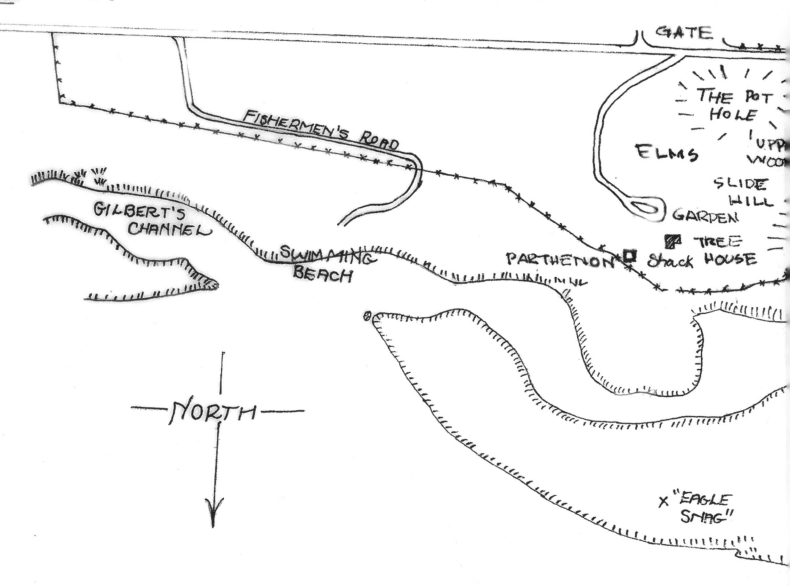

MR. COLEMAN
FOOD PATCH

TO GILBERT'S

THE PRAIRIE

GATE

THE POT
HOLE

UPPER
WOODS

ELMS

SLIDE
HILL

GARDEN

FISHERMEN'S ROAD

GILBERT'S
CHANNEL

SWIMMING
BEACH

PARTHENON

TREE
Shack HOUSE

NORTH

X "EAGLE
SNAG"